RIC&RAC's
Woodland Adventure

◆ ◆ ◆

H. Norman Wright
with **Gary J. Oliver**
Illustrated by Sharon Dahl

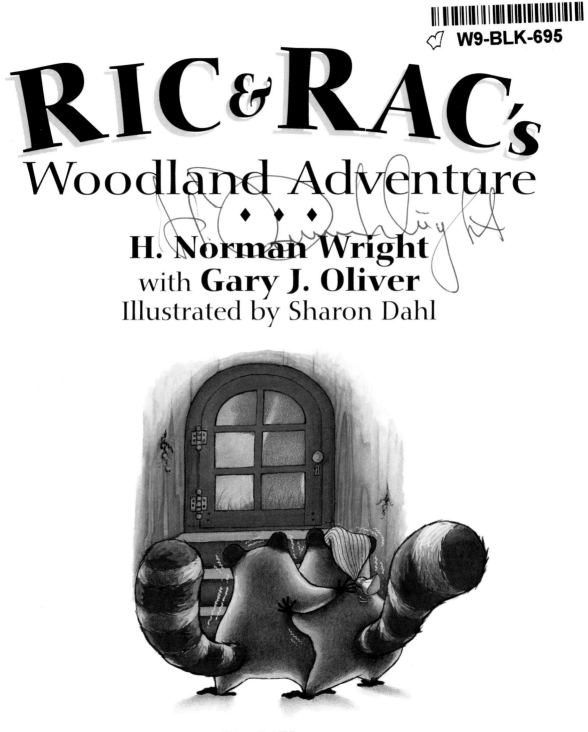

Chariot VICTOR
PUBLISHING
A DIVISION OF COOK COMMUNICATIONS

Ric woke up to the sound of scratchy noises and thumps outside the den he shared with his brother. Poking Rac, he whispered, "Wake up! I'm scared!"

"What's there to be scared of?" asked Rac, with a yawn.

Just then a dark shadow darkened their doorway. "That's what there is to be scared of," said Ric. He tried to hide behind his big brother.

Thump, thump, thump. The old tree above the den shook as bark fell off. The leaves shivered and the roots quivered. Ric dug his sharp nails into Rac's fur.

"**O**uch!" said Rac. "Calm down. Remember that song we learned in Raccoon School?" He sang:

> *"Fear can be a friend or fear can be a foe.*
> *That's something everyone needs to know."*

Under his breath, Ric mumbled, "Ho, ho, ho." He didn't see how fear could be his friend. He didn't like to feel scared.

"Look!" said Rac, peeking out of the den. "It's only Buford Bear. He's hitting our tree to drive the bees away from their hive."

"**W**atch out," Ric said. "Those bees are mad and they could sting."

"Right, brother. Being a little afraid of bees makes us more careful. That kind of fear is our friend."

Just then Buford saw them. "My, my. Are you two coming out to help me get some honey?"

"Oh, no," said Ric. "Bees sting. They can hurt. Aren't you afraid of them?"

"Me, afraid? I'm big and strong. Why should I be afraid?"

"You mean you're never afraid, Buford?" asked Rac.

"Nope. Never."

"**B**oo!" said Ric, sneaking up from behind.

"Ah-h-h-o-o-o-w!" howled Buford.

Ric laughed. "See, I scared you!"

"No, a bee stung me," replied the bear. "O-w-w-w! Maybe I should have been more careful." And with that, Buford lumbered away.

"I don't believe Buford Bear," said Ric. "Isn't everybody afraid sometime, Rac?"

"**Y**es. But some—like Buford—don't want to admit they get scared. Others are afraid too much. They are scared of things they don't really need to worry about. That's when fear is a *foe*—getting in our way and making us unhappy." Rac thought a minute. "Ric, I'm going to take you to meet somebody like that. She lives on the far side of the woods. Are you afraid to come with me?"

"No!" said Ric. But his voice had a funny squeak in it. He had never been to the far side of the woods.

Through the forest the raccoon brothers went. They squeezed under fallen trees, swam across the stream, climbed over trees, and scrabbled through hollowed-out logs. Finally they came to the edge of the woods. But just as they stepped into the sunlight, a loud screech filled the air. Ric and Rac looked at each other, then raced back into the dark forest.

As soon as Rac found a hollow log, he jumped inside. Ric followed close behind. Safe inside, the little raccoon took a deep breath. "Pew!" he sputtered, "What's that awful smell?"

"Yuck!" said Rac, holding his nose. "I can't stand it!"

"It doesn't bother me," said a new voice.

"Who's that?" asked Rac.

"Hey, boys! It's me!" The new voice echoed in the darkness.

Ric and Rac looked through a knothole in the log and saw two yellow eyes.

"Who—are you?" asked Rac, his voice trembling.

The two eyes blinked. "It's me. Boo!"

The startled raccoons jumped out of the log and ran into the maze of trees. They quickly lost each other, scrambling in opposite directions to get away from those scary eyes.

"**R**ic!" called Rac.

"Rac!" called Ric.

Suddenly Ric realized he was alone in the woods.

Suddenly Rac realized he was alone in the woods.

Then Rac started to sing loudly, *"Fear can be a friend or fear can be a foe. It's something everyone needs to know."*

Ric heard the song, faintly at first. Then he sang an answer as loud as he could, *"Fear can be a friend or fear can be a foe."*

As the brothers listened and sang, they found each other at last—right back at the log where they started. They looked around for those scary, yellow eyes.

Suddenly, out of the log popped Smelly the Skunk. "Hi, guys! Boy, did I scare you. Ha, ha!"

"Ah–h–h–h, we knew it was you all the time," said Rac.

"Sure," said Smelly. "Well, I'm going back to smell... I mean *sleep*. Drop in again sometime."

"Rac, you were just as scared as I was, weren't you?"

"Yes. But that kind of fear wasn't good. If we had stopped and looked, we would have seen it was only Smelly."

"Well, when we ran from the screech before, at the edge of the woods, was that an all-right kind of fear?" asked Ric.

"I think so. It was an eagle, and they like to eat little raccoons like us. So our fear helped us look for safety. And now little brother, let's get back to the edge of the woods. I still want you to meet somebody."

Back through the woods they went. Finally, in a towering tree, they found a jittery looking creature who never stopped moving.

"Excuse us, Shirl Squirrel."

"Oh! You surprised me! What is it? I'm busy you know. I'm always busy."

"We have a question. Are you ever afraid?"

"**M**e? Afraid? I'm always afraid. You know what I'm afraid of? I'll tell you. I'm afraid of the other animals not liking me. What if they laugh at me? What if they chase me? What if . . . what if . . . what if? Oh me! I'm afraid of new things, loud things, strange things. I'm so afraid of fear, I don't know what to do. That's why I run around in circles, and up and down, you know. Oh dear, oh dear, I live my life full of fear."

Ric and Rac looked at each other and crept away while Shirl was still talking.

"She lives with all those fears. That's no fun," Ric said.

"Right. Those aren't friendly fears. She doesn't have any real reason to be so afraid all the time. Many of her fears are in her own imagination. If she would stop and think, or ask questions, she wouldn't be so afraid."

"But some fears are good, right?"

"Uh huh. If there's danger and you feel scared, that's good—because it keeps you from getting hurt. That's when fear is our friend."

Just then Ric heard a loud growl. He jumped!

But then he held himself very still and listened.
When he heard the growl again, he laughed. It was his
stomach, telling him it was time to go home for supper!

The raccoon brothers made their way through the forest again.

After a big supper of water snails, crayfish, and mushrooms, Ric lay
down for a long day's rest. Suddenly he woke to the sound of loud
scratching back and forth, right by the doorway of the den.

"Oh, no!" he thought. "Maybe something is trying to get through our
door! Or maybe a human is sawing down our tree."

Ric's heart started to beat faster and his paws got sweaty. His eyes
grew bigger, his tummy turned over, and he started to think. "What if . . .
what if. . . . "

He suddenly slapped his paw loudly on the ground and told himself,
"Stop that!"

He made such a noise that Rac woke up sputtering, "What's that?
What's happening?"

Ric took a deep breath, then bravely walked to the door. *"Fear can be a friend, or fear can be a foe. It's something I'm finally starting to know."* He sang the little song quietly to himself. As he walked, he felt less afraid. His heart didn't beat as fast and his tummy felt calmer.

He poked his head out the door and what did he see? Elwood Elk— shining his antlers on the side of the tree.

Elwood stopped when he saw Ric and said, "Oh, please excuse me." He turned away, looking very proper and proud.

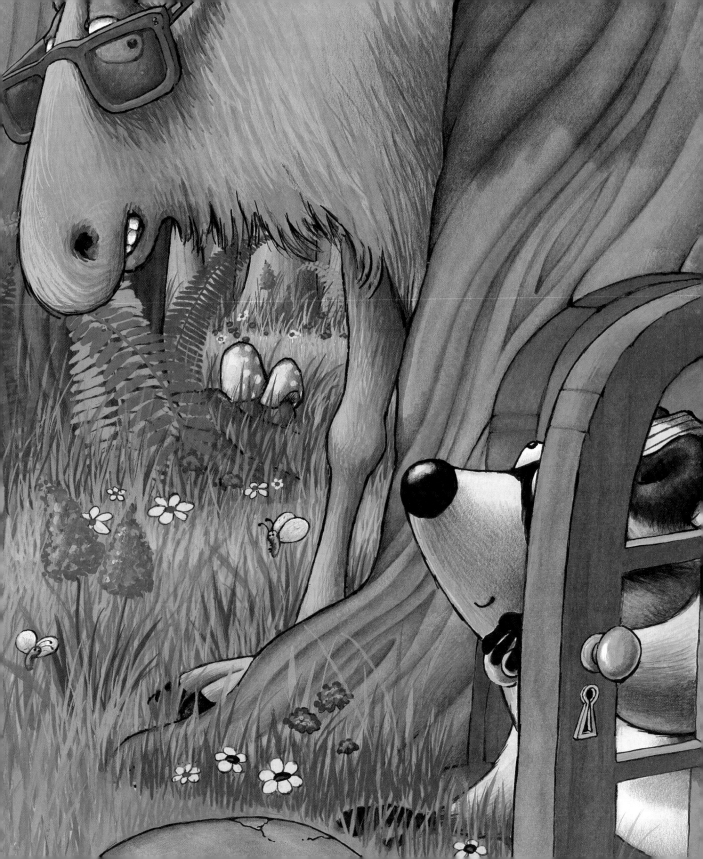

Ric smiled, sighed, and settled back inside his den. He told his brother, "Go back to sleep, Rac. It's nothing to be scared of. I found out what the noise was and took care of it. Isn't it great that we don't have to be afraid of every little thing?"

And with that he snuggled down and fell into a deep sleep.

GROWING ON:
HOW GROWNUPS CAN HELP A CHILD COPE WITH FEAR

Ask your child to give you his or her definition of fear. Ask: *Do you think fear is good or bad? Where did you learn that?*

Explain that fear is a God–given emotion which everyone experiences. There are different ways to express the fear that all of us experience. Some ways are helpful and some do harm.

Talk about these questions:

★ Ask your child to talk to you about his or her fears.

☾ Share what scared you when you were a child. Describe what you did that helped you overcome your fears.

★ Read Proverbs 3:24–26 to your child: "When you lie down, you will not be afraid; when you lie down, your sleep will be sweet. Have no fear of sudden disaster or of the ruin that overtakes the wicked, for the Lord will be your confidence and will keep your foot from being snared."
(If your child struggles with fear or worry, read this passage to him or her each night at bedtime. Help your child learn it by heart.)

☾ Talk with your child about what things it's good to be afraid of and what we don't have to be frightened about.

★ Talk together about specific things your child can do when he or she is afraid.

☾ Together, read the following Bible passages: "So do not fear, for I am with you; do not be dismayed, for I am your God. I will strengthen you and help you," (Isaiah 41:10).